Beauty and The Beast

Once upon a time there was a rich man who had three daughters. Suddenly, almost overnight, he lost nearly all his money. The family had to sell their grand house and move to a tiny run-down cottage in the country.

The two older girls were always complaining about having to patch their dresses and never being able to go to parties. But the youngest, who was called Beauty because of her sweet face and gentle nature, made the best of everything.

One day, their father set off to town to see if he could find work. As he mounted his horse, he asked the girls what they would like if he earned enough money to buy them each a present.

"A beautiful dress for me!" said the first daughter.

"A silver necklace!" said the second.

"Just come back safely, Papa," said Beauty. "That's enough for me."

"Oh Beauty! There must be *something* you would like!"

"A red rose for my hair then," she said with a smile. "But it's winter, so I won't mind if you can't find me one."

"I'll do my best for all of you," said their father, and he galloped away.

But he had a miserable time in town. There was no work anywhere. The only gifts he could afford were fruit and chocolate for the older girls, and there were no flowers at all for Beauty. Then, on the way home, his horse went lame and he had to dismount.

A snowstorm blew up and the unlucky man found himself hopelessly lost in the middle of a dark wood. Suddenly, he saw through the blizzard a high wall and a pair of locked, wrought-iron gates. At the end of the drive he could see a huge mansion with warm lights in the windows.

"If only I could shelter here." No sooner had he spoken than the gates swung open. The stormy wind suddenly swept him up the drive to the steps of the house. The door creaked open, revealing a candlelit table set with the most tempting food and drink.

He glanced back down the drive through the swirling snow, and saw that the gates had silently closed and his horse was gone. He stepped inside, and the door creaked shut behind him.

While he was gazing nervously round the room, one of the chairs pulled itself back from the table, clearly inviting him to sit down. "Well, I'm obviously welcome here!" he thought. "I might as well enjoy myself!"

When he had eaten and drunk as much as he could, he noticed a big sofa in front of the fire, with a fur rug spread across the seat. A corner of the rug turned back as if to say, "Do come and lie down." So that's what he did.

The next thing he knew, it was morning. He got up feeling wonderful and sat down at the table where breakfast was waiting for him. There was even a red rose in a silver vase on the table.

"A red rose!" he exclaimed. "What a stroke of luck. Beauty will have her present after all." He ate as much as he could, stood up and took the rose out of its slender vase.

At once, a terrible roar filled the air. The fire in the grate shrank back against the chimney and all the candles flickered. The outer door burst open. There, framed against the snowy garden, was the most horrifying sight.

Was it a man or a beast? It was dressed in gentlemen's clothes — but there were hairy claws where there should have been hands, and its head was a mass of tangled fur.

"Steal my rose, would you?" it snarled, showing its appalling fangs. "What kind of thanks is that for the hospitality I've given you?"

The man nearly died of fright. "Please forgive me, sir. It was for my daughter, Beauty. But I'll put it back at once of course."

"Too late!" growled the Beast. "You must take it with you now . . . and send me your daughter in exchange."

"No!" gasped Beauty's father. "No!"

"Then I shall eat you this minute," roared the Beast.

"Better for you to eat me than my lovely daughter," said the unhappy man.

"If you send her, I'll not harm a hair of her head,"

said the Beast. "You have my word on it. Now, choose."

The girl's father agreed to the dreadful bargain, and the Beast gave him a magic ring which, if twisted three times, would bring Beauty to the Beast's desolate mansion.

Outside in the snow stood the horse, now cured of its lameness, saddled and ready for the journey. But what a miserable journey it was, and an even worse homecoming when he told his daughters what had happened.

"Did he really say he would not hurt me, father?" asked Beauty.

"He gave his word, my darling."

"Then give me the ring," said Beauty. "Don't forget me, will you everyone?" She kissed them goodbye, put

on the ring, and twisted it three times.

Almost at once, she found herself in the Beast's mansion.

But he was not there to greet her. In fact she did not see him at all for many days, but the house made her very welcome. Doors opened by themselves, candlesticks floated upstairs to guide her to bed, food appeared at the table and was mysteriously cleared away.

Beauty was not frightened by the friendly house, but she felt so lonely that she began to wish the Beast would come and talk to her — however awful he looked.

One day, as she wandered in the garden, the Beast stepped out from behind a tree. Beauty could not stop herself giving a scream as she covered her eyes.

"Don't be afraid, Beauty," he murmured, trying to keep the growl out of his voice. "I've only come to wish you good day and ask if you are enjoying your stay at my house."

"Well," said Beauty, taking a deep breath, "I'd rather be at home. But I am well looked after, thank you."

"Good," said the Beast. "Would you mind if I walked with you for a while?"

So the two of them wandered about the garden, and after that the Beast often came to talk to Beauty. But he never sat down to eat with her at the big table.

5

One night, Beauty saw him loping across the moonlit lawn. She realised with a shock that he was out hunting for his food. Glancing up, he saw her at the window. Covering his face with his great paws, he let out a roar of shame.

Although he was ugly, Beauty was so lonely and he was so kind to her that she began to look forward to seeing him.

One evening, he came up behind her when she was sitting reading by the fire. "Marry me, Beauty," he said.

He looked so hopeful that Beauty felt sorry for him. "I do like you *very* much, Beast, but no, I really don't want to marry you. I don't love you."

The Beast often repeated his polite offer of marriage. But she always said "No" as kindly as she possibly could.

One day he found her weeping by the fountain in the garden. "Oh Beast!" she cried. "I'm sorry to cry when you've been so kind to me, but it's almost

winter! I've been here nearly a year. I'm so homesick. I miss father, so much."

To her joy, Beast said, "You may go home for seven days if you promise to come back." Beauty promised at once, and twisted the ring on her finger.

What joy there was when Beauty appeared in the little kitchen in the middle of supper. They had a wonderful week together. Beauty told her family all about her strange host and they told her all their news. The happy week passed with no sign or word from the Beast. "Perhaps he's forgotten," thought Beauty. "I'll stay a bit longer." Another week passed and, to her delight, nothing happened at all. The family breathed a sigh of relief.

Then one night, as she was brushing her hair in front of the mirror, her reflection suddenly faded — and there instead was the Beast. He was lying by

the moonlit fountain, almost hidden by fallen leaves.

"Oh Beast!" exclaimed Beauty, tears springing to her eyes. "Please don't be dead. I'll come back. Dear Beast."

She twisted the ring three times and found herself by his side in the garden.

"Beast, oh Beast," she wept, lifting his huge head on to her lap. "I didn't mean to kill you. I love you."

She tried to brush the leaves from his face, but her eyes were so full of tears that she could not see, and tears brimmed over and splashed down on to his head.

Suddenly, he spoke. "Look at me, Beauty. Wipe away your tears and see what you have done."

Beauty looked down and saw that she was stroking a head of golden hair. Beast had vanished and in his place was the most handsome of men.

"Who are you?" she gasped. The young man took her face in his hands.

"I am a prince," he said. "A witch cast a spell on me to change me into a beast forever. Only the true love of a young girl could free me. Ah Beauty, I'm so glad you came back. *Now* will you marry me?"

"Of course, my Prince, I will." And the two of them lived happily ever after.

Alan Baker

THE HAPPY PRINCE

High above the city, on a tall stone column, stood the beautiful statue of the Happy Prince. His body was covered in thin leaves of fine gold, his eyes were two sparkling sapphires, and a large red ruby glowed in his sword-hilt.

"How happy the Prince looks," the townspeople would say, as they wandered through the square. "What a pity we can't all be happy like him."

One night, a swallow flew over the city. Winter was coming, and he was flying south to the warmth and sunshine, charting his course by the stars. All the other swallows had gone weeks before, but this one had lingered behind. Now he was hurrying to join his friends before the snows arrived.

When the swallow saw the golden prince at the top of the stone column, he stopped to take a rest. "What a wonderful statue," he thought. "I'll perch between its feet to keep out of this wind."But just as he was folding his wings, a large drop of water splashed down beside him. "Rain? On such a clear, starry night?"

A second drop fell. Then another. The swallow shook his feathers irritably. "What use is a statue if it doesn't keep the rain off!" Then he looked up at the Prince and what did he see? The drops were not rain at all, but tears, trickling slowly down from the Prince's golden cheeks.

"Who are you?" asked the swallow, full of wonder.

"I am the Happy Prince."
"Then why are you weeping?"
"Because of what I see," answered the statue. "When I was alive, and had a human heart, I did not know what tears were — I was always rich and happy. My courtiers loved me so much that when I died, they made me into a statue. Then they placed me on this pedestal, high above the city. From here I can see all the ugliness and misery of the city. And though my heart now is made of lead I cannot help but weep."

Three more tears rolled down the Princes's face. Then he spoke again. "In a little street on the dark side of town, a poor woman spends each day sewing at the window of her house. Her face is thin and tired. Her body is racked with grief. Her little boy lies in bed in the corner. He has a fever, and is crying out for oranges. But his mother is so poor that she can give him nothing but water.

"Please, dear Swallow, help me. Take the ruby from my sword and give it to her."

"But I'm on my way to Egypt," said the swallow. "I must fly on, right away. All my friends are waiting for me, and the snows will soon arrive."

"Just help me for one night," the Prince pleaded, "and be my messenger. The boy is so thirsty — and his mother is so sad."

So the swallow picked out the ruby from the Prince's sword and flew over the rooftops to the little house.

back to the Happy Prince to say goodbye.

"Can you not stay one more night, little Swallow?"

"My friends are waiting for me, and the winter is almost here. How can I stay?"

"On the dark side of the city, there is a young man hunched over a desk. He's trying to write, but the fire has gone out

The poor woman was so tired that she had fallen asleep over her sewing. She did not stir when the bird hopped through the window and laid the ruby down by her thimble. The little boy tossed and turned on his bed, burning with fever. The swallow fanned his hot cheeks with his wings, then flew back to the Prince.

"It's strange," he said, "but although it is so cold I feel much warmer now."

"That's because you have done a kind deed," replied the Prince. And the swallow slept peacefully.

Next day the swallow flew around the town, admiring the sights. When he passed the poor woman's house, he saw that the boy was over his fever, and was standing at the window with a basket full of oranges. "Look Mummy — a swallow, so close to winter." His mother hugged her son and smiled.

As night drew in, and the stars appeared to guide him, the swallow flew

and he's too poor to buy
fuel. His fingers are too cold to
grip the pen. Pluck out one of my
sapphire eyes and take it to him."

"Oh Prince," the swallow gasped, "I
cannot do that!" And he began to weep.

"Swallow, Swallow, little Swallow! Do
as I command."

So the swallow plucked out the Prince's
eye and flew to the writer's house. The poor
young man was sitting at his desk, with his
head in his hands and heard nothing when
the swallow fluttered through a hole in the
roof. The little bird placed the jewel on the
table, then departed as quietly as he had
arrived.

Raising his head from his hands, the
young man saw the precious sapphire and
gasped with surprise. "What's this! I must
have a secret admirer! Oh, now I can buy
wood for the fire — and finish my story!"

The next day, the swallow watched the
ships in the harbour preparing to set sail.
His heart sang for joy. "Tonight I am going
to Egypt!" he cried — but nobody heard.
And when the moon rose he flew back to
the Happy Prince. "I have come to say
goodbye!"

"What a pretty piece of glass," she said, and ran home laughing.

The swallow felt so warm and happy that he flew back to the Prince and said, "You are blind now. I will stay with you always."

"No, little Swallow," said the poor Prince. "Go away to Egypt."

"I will stay with you always," said the swallow, and slept at the Prince's feet.

All next day he sat on the Prince's shoulder, and told him stories of the strange lands he had seen. The Prince listened and then said, "Fly over my city, little Swallow, and tell me what you see!"

So the swallow flew over the city and saw the rich people in their beautiful houses, eating and dancing and laughing. Then he flew over the drab streets where the poor people lived, and saw the starving children huddled together for warmth.

"Swallow, little Swallow, stay with me just one more night," said the Prince.

"But it's almost winter, and the snows are coming! I *must* fly to Egypt and join my friends — if I don't go now, there will be nowhere left for me to build my nest!"

The Prince was silent for a moment, then he said, "There is a little match-girl down there in the square. She hasn't sold any matches all day, and when she goes home her father will beat her. She has no stockings or shoes, and her little head is bare. Pluck out my other eye and give it to her!"

"I will stay here with you one more night — but I cannot pluck out your eye! You would be blind."

"Swallow, little Swallow, do as I command."

So the bird plucked out the Prince's other eye, and swooped down to the match-girl. He dropped the shimmering sapphire into her palm and she looked at it with joy.

When he told the Prince what he had seen, the Prince said, "I am covered in fine gold. You must pick it off, leaf by leaf and take it to the poor."

So the swallow picked away the gold, leaf by leaf, until the Happy Prince looked dull and grey. Then he carried it to the poor. As he dropped the gold at the children's feet, the swallow was gladdened to see their faces grow rosier, and hear their happy laughter.

Then the snow fell, soft and heavy on the rooftops. The swallow grew colder and colder and flapped his wings to keep warm. He would not leave the Prince, for he loved him dearly, but he knew he was going to die. He just had the strength to fly up to the Prince's shoulder one last time.

"Are you going south at last, little Swallow? You've stayed far too long. Kiss me before you go, for I love you."

"I cannot fly to Egypt, Prince," said the swallow. "I am going to die." And he kissed the Happy Prince on the lips and fell dead to the ground — a bundle of crumpled feathers in the wind.

At that moment, there was a sharp crack. The Prince's leaden heart had broken in two.

Early next morning, the mayor and the town councillors were walking by when they paused to look up at the statue.

"Oh dear," said the mayor. "Just look at the Happy Prince. The ruby's gone from his sword, his eyes are missing, and his gold has peeled off. What can have happened? He looks no better than a beggar. And what's this dead bird doing here? Throw it on the rubbish heap and put up a notice: *Birds are forbidden to die here.* It really is too bad!"

They pulled down the statue of the Happy Prince and melted him down in a furnace — to make a new statue, of the mayor.

But the Prince's leaden heart would not melt in the furnace. "That's strange," said the foreman when he found it, and he tossed it carelessly on the rubbish heap, beside the dead swallow.

"Bring me the two most precious things in the city," said God to one of his angels. And the angel returned with the leaden heart and the dead bird.

"You have made the right choice," said God. "For in my garden of Paradise, this tiny bird will sing for ever, and the Happy Prince will live in my city of gold."

DICK WHITTINGTON and his CAT

Dick Whittington woke one morning with a hankering for adventure. He bounded out of the house and on to the village green.

"Hey!" an old farmer called to the boy, "you ought to take yourself off to London. It's too quiet round here for the likes of you. They do say that the streets there be paved with gold."

Dick was amazed. "Gold! Then just one cobblestone would make me rich!"

"But then again, I never believe what town folk say," added the farmer, laughing.

But he was too late to stop Dick. The

young man had two words ringing in his ears: 'London' and 'gold'. "And now to the city," he cried, "to make my fortune!"

The first signpost outside the village said 'London'. "Good," thought Dick, "it must be just over the hill." But London was not just over the hill; nor over the next, nor the next. Exhausted, Dick lay down to sleep in the shelter of an old oak tree.

In the middle of the night he was awakened by a tickling on his cheek. Sitting up, he saw a marmalade cat smiling at him. "Excuse me, sir," said the cat, "but have you got a saucer of milk to spare?"

"I'm sorry," said Dick. "All the food and drink I set off with has gone, and I've no money to buy more".

"Never mind," said the cat. "If we curl up together at least we'll be warm."

of London. The roads were suddenly busy. Everybody seemed to be shouting and hurrying, pushing and quarrelling. But the streets were not paved with gold — they were running with mud.

Dick and Tom ducked out of the way of the thronging crowds, and ran through an arch and into a courtyard. Dick knocked on the basement door of a grand-looking house. "Er, have you got a job for a hard-working country boy?" he shouted.

A fearsome face as white as dough and crowned with fiery red hair appeared round

And that is how Dick made friends with his cat, who very soon told him that his name was Tom. In the morning they travelled on together towards London. On and on they walked until at last Dick said, "I'm going back, Tom. I've had enough. There can't be anything in London that's worth all this walking." And he turned his back on London and began trudging home.

At that very moment the sound of bells began to ring across the fields. They were the church bells of the City of London and they seemed to be singing:

"Turn again Whittington,
Lord Mayor of London!"

Over and over again they chimed, until the words jangled in Dick's head.

"You can't give up now!" cried Tom. "Onwards to London!"

And there it lay, round the next corner, the gleaming, smoking, ramshackle chaos

the door. "Come in 'ere, boy, and scrape the pots. I'm cook in this house. If you work hard, I might let you eat the scrapings!"

And that was how Dick came to work in the house of Captain Fitzwarren. He worked so hard scraping and polishing that by evening he wanted only to sleep. But the mice that infested his attic bedroom kept him awake — until one night he said to Tom, "Go get 'em, boy!" And the mice ran for their lives. Dick's cat was a great comfort to him.

So, too, was Captain Fitzwarren's young daughter, Alice. She would often come down to the kitchen to sit and talk with Dick.

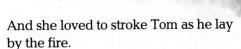

And she loved to stroke Tom as he lay by the fire.

"If I were Lord Mayor of London," Dick used to say laughingly, "I'd marry you, Alice Fitzwarren." And Alice would smile and say, "If you did become Lord Mayor of London, of course I'd marry you." And the cat would purr and say, "Who knows? Who knows?"

One day, Captain Fitzwarren announced that he was setting sail on a voyage. He gathered together his family and servants, and said goodbye to them all. When he noticed Dick standing beside the cook, his cat in his arms, he said, "Now that's just what I need. Here's a silver shilling, boy, for your cat. He's a ship's cat now."

Dick tried to protest, but the cook smacked him sharply. "Do as you're told, and don't argue with the master!" Dick returned sadly to his chilly attic, but it was so lonely without Tom that he decided to go and fetch him back. Just before dawn, he crept up the gangplank of the ship, little knowing that it was just about to sail.

And *that* is how Dick came to be cabin boy aboard Captain Fitzwarren's ship, and to sail to the mysterious lands of the East.

After weeks in storm-tossed waters, the ship ran aground on a strange, uncharted shore. Strange, warlike soldiers escorted the ship's company to the Sultan Suleiman's palace — cargo, cat and all.

"Mighty Suleiman!" said Fitzwarren spreading the entire ship's cargo before him, "I bring a few humble possessions in the hope of pleasing your Eminence."

"Hmm," said the Sultan. "I have every possession a man could desire. What need have I of these trinkets?"

As the Sultan spoke, Dick could not help but notice that the whole palace was overrun with mice and rats. Tom wriggled restlessly in Dick's arms. "Rrrow! rrow! I can't bear it another minute!"

Leaping out of Dick's arms, he pounced towards the Sultan's daughter, the Sultana, dived under her throne, and came out dragging a huge rat in his jaws!

"O Sun and Moon!" shrieked the Sultana. "What wonderful beast is this?"

Tom ran round the palace, scattering mice and rats, and swallowing a dozen or more. "O marvellous beast!" cried the Sultan. "During my reign and the reign of my father, this country has been plagued with rats. But this creature is a veritable slayer of rats! Name your price, Captain! For this creature I will pay a sack of diamonds!"

Dick caught Tom up in his arms. "Oh, but he's my friend, sir. I couldn't leave him behind in a foreign land!"

The cat whispered in Dick's ear. Dick set him down on the floor and off he ran towards the ship. "He will return," said Dick. Impatiently the Sultan waited. Anxiously Dick and the Captain watched the door for the cat's return. At last a small, whiskered face peeped round the door, and Tom returned — leading a family of kittens! At once they began pouncing on mice.

"You have always had cats in your country," said Tom. "But they were frightened by your warlike ways. These six would be most proud and honoured to serve you and your son, and your son's sons — as long as you put away your swords. And now, if it please your Excellency, I'd like to go home with my friend Dick."

The Sultan clapped his hands with delight. "O Earth and Sky! but this is wonderful! I have six rat-slayers instead of one! Great must be the reward for those who brought me these cat-beasts! To the boy Dick I offer my daughter — yes, my own daughter — for a wife. You aren't married, are you boy?"

Dick bowed very low. "No, your Gloriousness, but I have sworn to marry none other than the beautiful Alice Fitzwarren, daughter of this worthy sea-captain." The Sultan was disappointed, and the Sultana was *very* disappointed. But they comforted themselves by giving Dick three sacks of diamonds and a turban.

"O most generous Suleiman!" said Dick. "Our boat is grounded on your beautiful shores, and without help we can never return home."

"Not another word!" cried the Sultan. "Here are two flying carpets woven by my own magician — one for the ship's crew and another for my humble gift of treasure."

And *that* is how Dick Whittington came home to London. As the two carpets swooped over the roof of the house, Alice looked out of her window and waved.

"Dick!" cried the Captain, climbing off the carpet, "now that you've made your fortune, you're as good a husband as I could wish for my Alice. And what's more, I do believe she's in love with you. Why not run and ask her?"

"Do you remember my promise?" said Alice. "I vowed to marry you if ever you became Lord Mayor of London."

Such was his love for Alice that Dick immediately set to work. Using the treasure given him by the Sultan he soon became a rich and successful merchant. He was hard-working, popular and fair; and before two years had passed he was elected Lord Mayor of London.

On the day of the wedding the streets were filled with people, all agog to see the new Lord Mayor and his beautiful bride.

Tom sat beside Dick and Alice in their golden coach, wearing a new ribbon with a bright silver bell.

But no-one could hear it ringing above the huge pealing chimes of the bells of the City of London, as they rang out:

"Hail Richard Whittington
Lord Mayor of London."

SNOW WHITE
and the
seven dwarfs

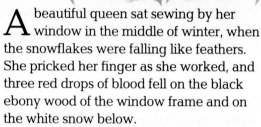

A beautiful queen sat sewing by her window in the middle of winter, when the snowflakes were falling like feathers. She pricked her finger as she worked, and three red drops of blood fell on the black ebony wood of the window frame and on the white snow below.

"I wish for a daughter with skin as white as snow, lips as red as blood and hair as black as ebony," she sighed.

And so it happened. She had a little girl with skin as white as snow, with lips as red as blood and with hair as black as ebony. Her parents called her Snow White. But only a few days after her birth, her mother died.

Her father, the king, had truly loved his queen, but he needed a mother for Snow White, so he searched for a second wife.

He married a princess whose face was lovely as summer, but her heart was cold as ice and she worked dark magic. She was so vain she could not bear to think that anyone could be more beautiful than she was. When she came to the palace, the only thing she brought was a mirror in a golden frame. Each night, she whispered:

"Mirror, mirror, on the wall,
Who is the fairest one of all?"

And the mirror would answer:
"You, O Queen, are the fairest one by far!"

This made the new queen very happy, for she knew that the mirror could not lie. She preened herself in front of the glass and smiled in satisfaction.

But Snow White grew more and more beautiful every year until, one day, when she was seven, her wicked stepmother asked her usual question:

"Mirror, mirror, on the wall,
Who is the fairest one of all?"

This time the mirror replied:

"You, O Queen, are fair, and lovely too,
But Snow White is more fair than you!"

The queen was furious, and her lovely face turned ugly with rage. She called for her huntsman. "Take Snow White into the forest and kill her!" she screamed. "Cut out her heart and bring it to me as proof that you have done as I have ordered!"

Pale and trembling, the royal huntsman found Snow White playing in the garden, and grabbed her by the hand. Not once did he look at her. Not once did he speak.

Deep in the forest, he drew his dagger and held it to Snow White's heart. "Now you must die!"

But when she looked up at him, her red lips trembled and her black hair spilled around her shoulders.

"Let the wild beasts kill you," cried the huntsman. "I cannot!" And he ran off, leaving her alone in the forest.

On his way back to the palace, he killed a small fallow deer and cut out its heart. When he gave it to the cruel queen, he told her it was Snow White's heart. She gave a wild laugh and threw it to her dogs. "So much for Snow White!" she cried.

Snow White wandered lonely through the forest, frightened at shadows and fearful of strange sounds. But when the trees and bushes saw how lovely and afraid she was, they turned aside their thorns, and the sharp stones refused to cut her feet.

At dusk, she found a tiny house among the trees. There was no answer to her knock, so she pushed the door and went in.

What a funny little place it was! Everything was very neat. There was a checked cloth spread on the table, with seven loaves, and seven plates, seven knives, forks, spoons and goblets of wine, all laid out ready for supper. By the wall, there were seven beds, all in a row.

"I'm very hungry," thought Snow White, and she took a small bite from each piece of bread and then a sip of wine from each goblet. Then she tried each bed in turn.

"This bed is too long," she said, " . . . and this one is too short." But when she reached the seventh bed, it was just right. Soon, she was fast asleep.

The seven dwarfs who lived in the cottage returned at nightfall. They had been digging for gold in the mountains and were tired after their long day's work. They lit their candles and looked around the room.

"Who's been sitting on my stool?" said the first dwarf.

"And touching my plate?"

"And eating my bread?"

"And licking my spoon?"

"And using my fork?"

"And moving my knife?"

"And drinking my wine?" said the seventh and last dwarf.

The first dwarf went over to the bed by the wall. "Someone has been lying in my bed," he cried.

"And mine! And mine!" said the others.

"There is someone still sleeping in my bed," said the seventh and last dwarf.

They crowded round the bed to look.

"Less noise!" said the first dwarf.

"Keep those lights down!" said the second.

"Be careful not to wake her!" said the third.

So the last dwarf slept the night with the others, an hour in each bed.

Disguising herself as a pedlar, the wicked queen searched the forest until she found the cottage.

"Fine wares to sell!" she cried, as she knocked at the little door.

"Good morning," said Snow White. "Do you have some pretty things for me to buy?"

"I have laces, bobbins and ribbons of every colour of the rainbow," said the queen.

Snow White quite forgot the dwarfs' solemn warning as she let the visitor in.

"Gracious, child," the queen exclaimed. "How badly your bodice is laced! Let me do it," and she took a ribbon from her tray.

The pedlar threaded the ribbon, then pulled it tighter and tighter until the breath was squeezed out of Snow White's body and she fell down in a faint.

Snow White was very frightened when she woke up next morning and saw the dwarfs, but they listened to her story and were delighted she had come to stay.

"You can cook, can't you?" asked the first dwarf.

"And wash? And clean, and knit and spin?" asked the others.

"Then of course you must live with us," they chorused. "But remember — don't let anyone into the house while we are away."

For months, the queen thought that Snow White was dead, and she did not ask the mirror her question again until late one evening, when the king was away.

"Mirror, mirror, on the wall,
Who is the fairest one of all?"

The mirror replied:

"You, O Queen, are fair, and lovely too,
But Snow White's still more fair than you."

The queen's face turned black with rage, and she screamed in fury as she demanded where Snow White could be found.

The mirror sighed heavily and told her.

"So much for your beauty!" cackled the cruel queen. "Now you will die!"

"We're home!" called the dwarfs. But no-one answered. Snow White was as pale as death when they found her.

"Loosen her lace!" the dwarfs shouted in panic. When the first dwarf cut it, the life-giving air rushed into her lungs and Snow White quickly recovered.

"The queen will find out you're alive," they warned. "You mustn't let her in."

Of course, the queen soon found out that Snow White was not dead. Using all her magic powers, she prepared a very special apple. One side was green and safe to eat, the other side was red — and deadly poisonous.

"Apples!" she called, knocking at the cottage door. "Crisp, juicy apples!"

"Please go away," Snow White said, as she peeped through the window. "I'm not allowed to open the door to strangers."

"Wise girl," replied the queen as she took the poisoned apple from her basket and turned the green side to her lips to bite into it. "Here," she said. "Take the rest and enjoy it."

The apple did look extremely good. Snow White leaned out of the window and took the half which was red and juicy. She took one bite . . . and fell down dead.

"That's the end of you!" chortled the queen as she returned home in triumph.

At nightfall, the dwarfs came back from the mountain. "No!" cried the first dwarf, when he found Snow White.

"How empty our lives will be without her," they all said sorrowfully.

The dwarfs could not bury her in the cold dark earth, so they made a coffin of glass so that they could still see her. Then they made a golden plaque and wrote on it:

"Here lies Snow White, the daughter of a king."

They set the coffin on a green hill and guarded it day and night. Birds came to sing there. And animals came to sit there. The squirrels came first, then the rabbits and last a young fallow deer.

Snow White lay in her coffin for many years, and never once did the dwarfs leave her alone. Slowly she grew into a young woman, more beautiful than she had ever been.

At last a prince rode past and saw the coffin and the words written on the golden plaque.

"I would like to take her away with me," he said, but the dwarfs would not part with her.

"Will you take money?" he asked.

"She was worth more to us than all the gold in the world," the dwarfs replied.

"Then for sheer pity, let me kiss her once!" begged the prince. "For if she were alive, I would have loved her more than life itself!"

The dwarfs talked among themselves. "All right, just one kiss," they said, and opened the glass coffin.

But as the prince's lips touched the lips of Snow White, a piece of apple fell from her mouth and she opened her eyes.

"Where am I?"

"Safe," said the prince. And when Snow White looked into his face she could hardly believe what she saw.

"Your eyes are the colour of the sea. Your hair is as golden as the sun!"

The prince was overjoyed as he lifted her from the coffin. "I love you more than all the world. Marry me, and come with me to my father's kingdom."

And so Snow White said goodbye to the seven dwarfs, who had loved her so much. She thanked them, and promised that she would visit them often. Then she went with the prince to his father's castle where a great feast was prepared for their wedding.

Meanwhile the wicked queen preened herself in front of the magic mirror.

"Mirror, mirror, on the wall,
Who is the fairest one of all?"

The mirror gave a triumphant laugh:

"Your loathsome face is black as night,
Compared to the beauty of Snow White!"

"Aaargh!" screamed the queen, and tore the mirror off the wall and dashed it against the window sill. It shattered into a thousand pieces. A sliver of glass, as sharp as an icicle, pierced the queen's wicked heart and she fell down dead among the glittering fragments.

So the wicked queen never lived to see Snow White at her loveliest — riding at her father's side to her wedding in the palace chapel where her handsome prince awaited her.